For Helena, Rachael, Molly, Ella and Bella,
with love from H.M.

For Emily, A.H.

THERE'S A DRAGON DOWNSTAIRS
by Hilary McKay and Amanda Harvey

British Library Cataloguing in Publication Data
A catalogue record of this book is available from
the British Library.
ISBN 0 340 84141 9 (HB)

Text copyright © Hilary McKay 2003
Illustration copyright © Amanda Harvey 2003

First edition published 2003
10 9 8 7 6 5 4 3 2 1

Published by Hodder Children's Books
a division of Hodder Headline Limited
338 Euston Road London NW1 3BH

Colour Reproduction by Dot Gradations, UK
Printed in Hong Kong

There's a Dragon Downstairs

Written by Hilary McKay   Illustrated by Amanda Harvey

Hodder
Children's
Books

A division of Hodder Headline Limited

There was a dragon downstairs at Sophie's house.
Every night, Sophie heard him. Every night, he came,
rattling through the kitchen, slinking to the living room,
growing and growing in the dark.

Sophie's dad said, 'There is no dragon.
Not round here. Not in this house.'

Sophie's mum said, 'We'll go and look.'

They switched on all of the lights and looked in every room.

No dragon.

In the mornings, Sophie thought perhaps there was no dragon.

But, at night, she could still hear him.

It was very scary for Sophie, lying in bed, listening to the dragon rattle through the kitchen, slink to the living room, grow and grow in the dark.

That was why one night Sophie got out of bed,
put on her suit of armour,
picked up her shield,
and her very large sword,
and went downstairs to fight the dragon.

Sophie tried to creep very quietly down
the stairs, but you cannot creep dressed
as a knight in a suit of armour
with a shield and a very large sword.

Sophie clattered down the stairs...

…and into the living room.

No dragon.

In the morning Sophie thought
that was the end of the dragon downstairs.
The suit of armour and the shield and the
very large sword had frightened him away.

But, at night, he came again,
rattling through the kitchen,
slinking to the living room,
growing and growing in the dark.

This time Sophie did not put on
her suit of armour. She did not
want to fight the dragon.
But she did get out her fireman's
helmet and her pump-action
supersonic water squirter.
Because dragons breathe fire.

Very dangerous, thought Sophie,
breathing fire!
And she went downstairs to put
the dragon out.

Sophie tried to creep very quietly down the stairs, but you cannot creep with a fireman's helmet and a pump-action supersonic water squirter.

Sophie splashed downstairs...

...and into the living room.

No *dragon*.

In the morning Sophie thought that was the end of the dragon downstairs. The fireman's helmet and the pump-action supersonic water squirter had frightened him away.

But, at night, he came again,
rattling through the kitchen,
slinking to the living room,
growing and growing in the dark.

That night Sophie did not put on
her suit of armour. She did not
want to fight the dragon. She did
not take her fireman's helmet or
her pump-action supersonic water
squirter. She did not want to put
the dragon out.

She put on her crown and all of her jewels and
her long and floating princess dress.
Because dragons like princesses.
(To eat, thought Sophie, but he won't eat me!)
And she went downstairs to trick the dragon.

Sophie tried to creep very
quietly down the stairs,
but you cannot creep in a
long and floating princess dress.
Sophie fell downstairs and
into the living room.

No dragon.

In the morning Sophie thought, poor dragon. He thinks I am a pretend princess come to trick him.

He thinks I am a fireman come to put him out.

He thinks I am a knight in armour come to fight him.

He doesn't know I'm Sophie.

Sophie thought the dragon would never come back.

But, at night, he came again,
rattling through the kitchen,
slinking to the living room,
growing and growing in the dark.

This time Sophie did not put on anything.
She crept downstairs very quietly,
barefoot,
in the dark,
soundlessly to the living room,
gently, gently through the door…

THE DRAGON!

Sophie looked at the dragon, at last.
And the dragon looked at Sophie.
Then they ran to each other
like the best of friends.

And they were both still there…

…in the morning.